Extraordinary
JANE

Extraordinary ★ JANE ★

HANNAH E. HARRISON

DIAL BOOKS FOR YOUNG READERS AN IMPRINT OF PENGUIN GROUP (USA) LLC

To Lila Quinn,
the star of my circus

DIAL BOOKS FOR YOUNG READERS
Published by the Penguin Group * Penguin Group (USA) LLC, 375 Hudson Street, New York, NY 10014

USA | Canada | UK | Ireland | Australia | New Zealand | India | South Africa | China | penguin.com

A PENGUIN RANDOM HOUSE COMPANY

Library of Congress Cataloging-in-Publication Data
Harrison, Hannah E. * Ordinary Jane / Hannah E. Harrison.
p. cm. * Summary: "Jane the dog doesn't have a unique talent in the circus like the rest of her family, until the
ringmaster discovers what is truly special about her"—Provided by publisher.
ISBN 978-0-8037-3914-7 (hardcover : alk. paper) * [1. Dogs—Fiction. 2. Circus—Fiction. 3. Self-acceptance—
Fiction.] I. Title. PZ7.H2488Or 2014 [E]—dc23 2012009713

Special Markets ISBN 978-0-525-42995-1 NOT FOR RESALE
Manufactured in China on acid-free paper * 10 9 8 7 6 5 4 3 2
Designed by Jason Henry * Text set in Pueblo * The artwork for this book was created with acrylic paint on
bristol board. * The publisher does not have any control over and does not assume any responsibility for author
or third-party websites or their content.

DARE DEVIL SENSATIONS!

THE BOUFFANT BROS.

THRILLING

CANINE CANNONBALLS

LE GRAND CHAMPION

BRUTUS BOUFFANT
LE PLUS FORT
HERCULE DU MONDE

BICYCLES
TRICYCLES
SCOOTERS
& SKATES!

CIRCUS

BARNABY CIRCUS BELUCHI

The BOUFFANT SISTERS

HIGH WIRE ACT EXTRAORDINAIRE!

FURRY AND FEARLESS FEATS
THAT WILL AMAZE AND DELIGHT!

BARNABY BELUCHI

THE LOVELY LULA-BELLE

THE MOST GRACEFUL RIDER
THE WORLD HAS EVER KNOWN

CIRCUS

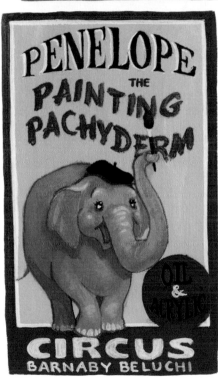

PENELOPE
THE
PAINTING
PACHYDERM

OIL
&
ACRYLIC

CIRCUS
BARNABY BELUCHI

BAR

AMAZ

SUPER

C

JANE was ordinary,

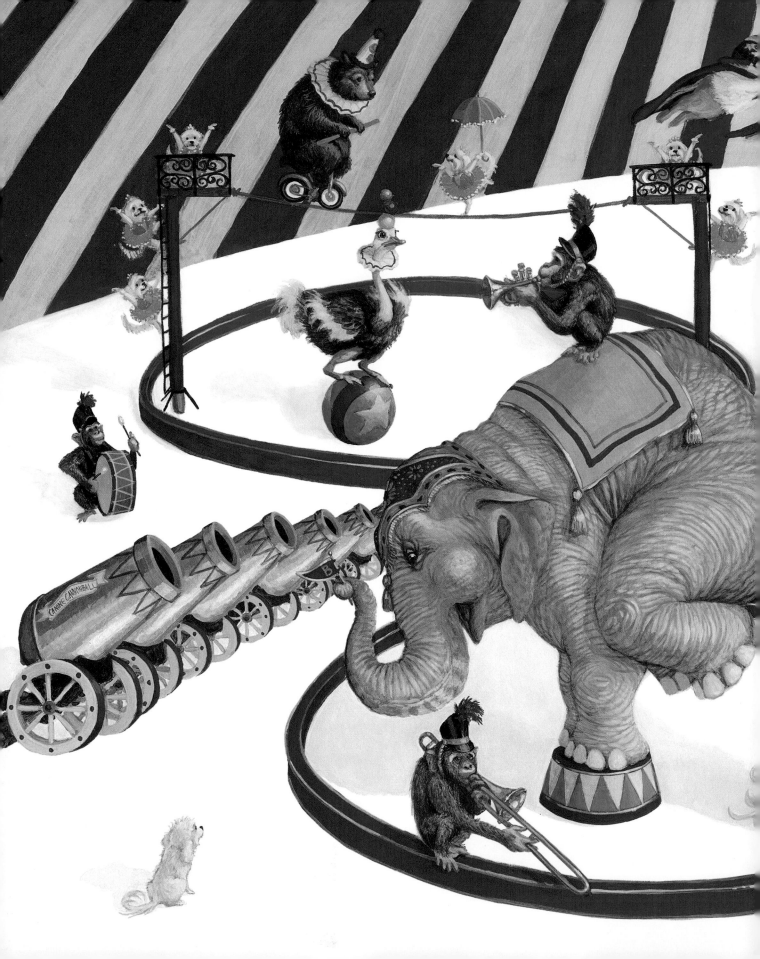

in a world that
was extraordinary.

She wasn't graceful
like her mother,

or mighty like her father.

She wasn't daring like her brothers,

or fearless like her sisters.

Jane was just Jane.

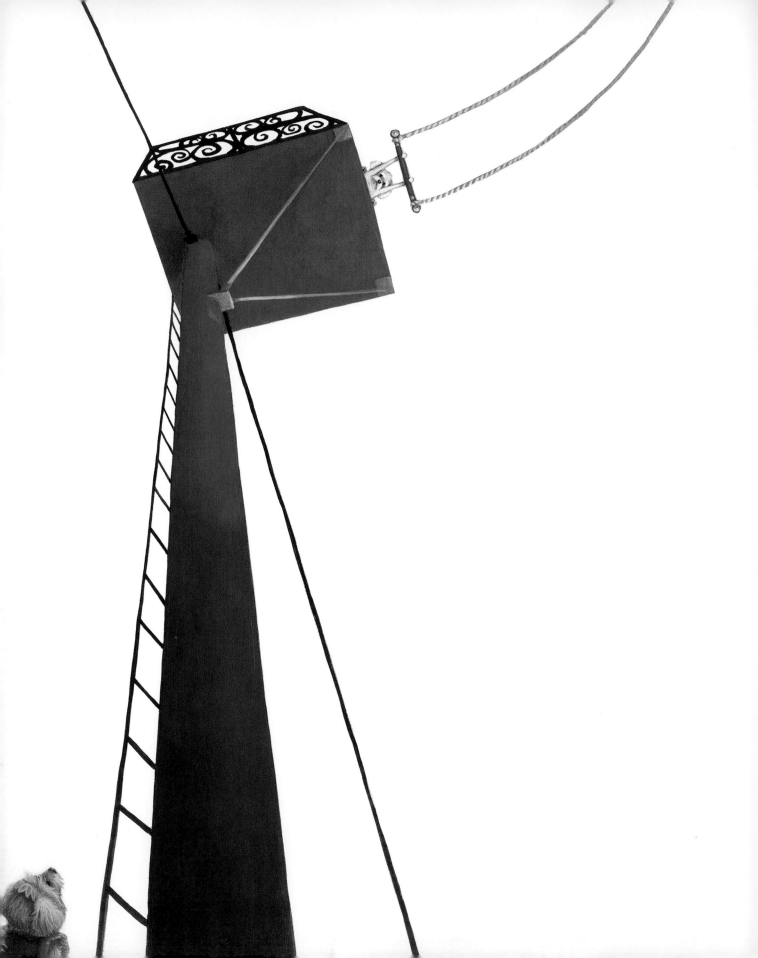

She tried to find her special talent.

But heights made her dizzy . . .

her jokes were a flop . . .

her music lacked
musicality . . .

her paintings,
pizzazz.

And then there was the
whole balancing ball disaster.

Jane . . .

was just . . .

Jane.

BARNABY BELUCHI'S

JANE

A REALLY GOOD DOG

CIRCUS

And that was enough.